Albert and Sarah Jane

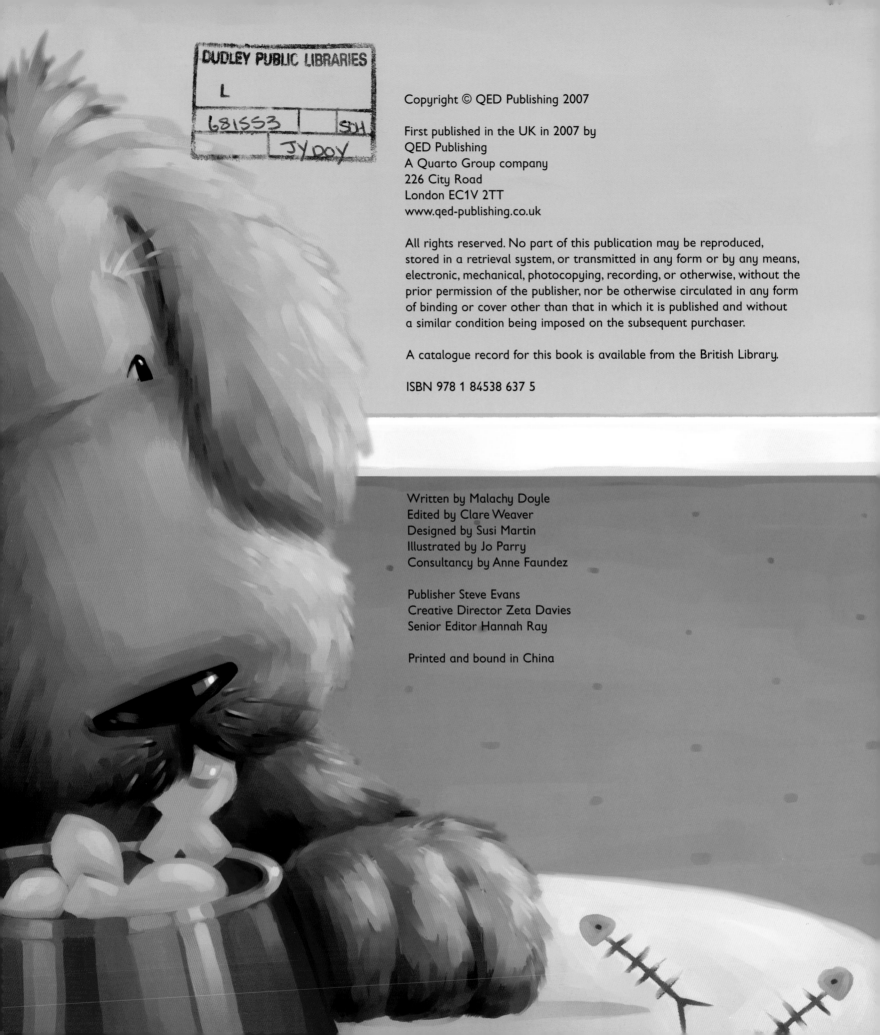

Copyright © QED Publishing 2007

First published in the UK in 2007 by
QED Publishing
A Quarto Group company
226 City Road
London EC1V 2TT
www.qed-publishing.co.uk

A catalogue record for this book is available from the British Library.

ISBN 978 1 84538 637 5

Written by Malachy Doyle
Edited by Clare Weaver
Designed by Susi Martin
Illustrated by Jo Parry
Consultancy by Anne Faundez

Publisher Steve Evans
Creative Director Zeta Davies
Senior Editor Hannah Ray

Printed and bound in China

Albert and Sarah Jane

Malachy Doyle

Illustrated by Jo Parry

QED Publishing

Albert and Sarah Jane were the very best of buddies.
Their favourite thing was to curl up in a great big
cat dog cuddle by the fire.

But there was one thing Albert liked even better than that.

And that was eating his yummy scrummy crunchies, from his big blue bowl.

And there was one thing he liked even better than **that**. And that was eating Sarah Jane's even yummier scrummier fishy nibbles.

He'd pinch one or two from her little red bowl, when his buddy wasn't looking, and they always tasted so much better than his own.

But one morning, while Sarah Jane was out and about early, Albert got a bit carried away with his nibbling.

mmmmmmm

So that when his pal came back in from the garden, all ready for breakfast, there wasn't a speck of food left in her little red bowl.

And when she looked to see if there was
anything in Albert's big blue bowl...

she found there wasn't
a speck of food there, either!

She went to ask him why they hadn't any food to eat,
but Albert was fast asleep in his basket.

That's odd, she thought, I'm sure he's fatter than usual.
And I'm sure he smells all fishy, too!

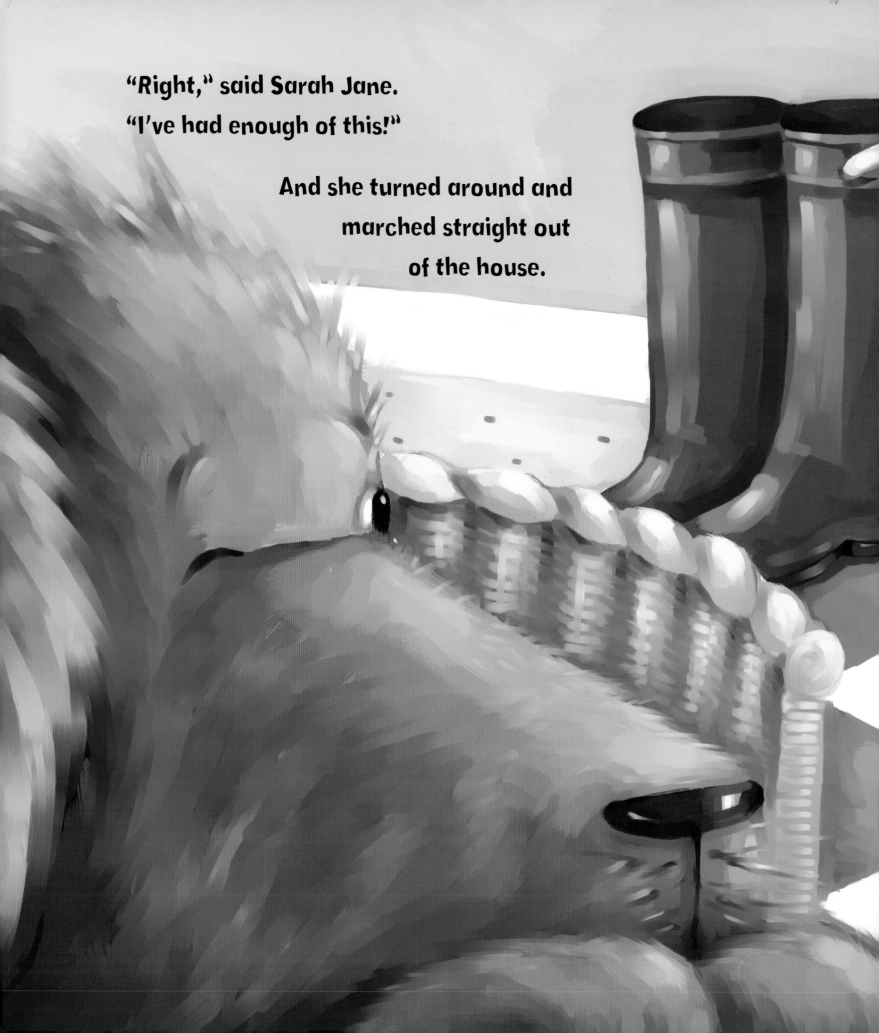

"Right," said Sarah Jane.
"I've had enough of this!"

And she turned around and
marched straight out
of the house.

Albert opened one eye, and
saw her going out of the cat flap.

She'll be back, he thought.
She always comes back.

But Sarah Jane didn't come back.
She went to live next door, instead.

By evening, Albert was lonely. By morning, he was howling at the cat flap.

"Come home, Sarah Jane!" he cried.

Albert spotted Sarah Jane
through the upstairs window.

He smiled at her, in a doggy
sort of way, but Sarah Jane
ignored him.

So, Albert slipped out of the house, went round to next door's doorstep, sat himself down by the cat flap, and howled.

"Come home, Sarah Jane!" he cried.

I miss you!

"Stop howling, you naughty dog!"
hissed Sarah Jane, coming down
to see what all the fuss was about.

"But I'm sad and lonely," said Albert.
"I want a great big cat dog cuddle by the fire."

"Well, the food's better over here, and nobody steals it," said Sarah Jane.

"But it's lonely here, too, without a big smelly lump of a dog to snuggle up to..."

"Me?" said Albert.

"Yes, you," said Sarah Jane.

"Do you miss me, too?" asked Albert.

"I do," said Sarah Jane.

"Well ... I'm sorry," said Albert.

"What for?" asked Sarah Jane.

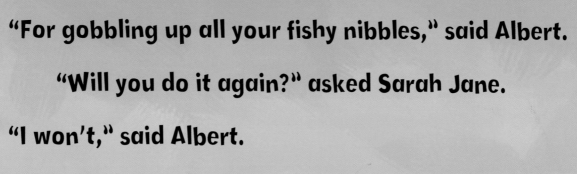

"For gobbling up all your fishy nibbles," said Albert.

"Will you do it again?" asked Sarah Jane.

"I won't," said Albert.

"Will you even nibble them?" asked Sarah Jane.

"I won't," said Albert.

"Good," said Sarah Jane.

So she marched back
into her very own house.
And Albert marched
in behind her.

They had a little nibble
from their red and
blue bowls...

And then they curled up together, in a great big cat dog cuddle by the fire, and fell asleep.

Notes for Teachers and Parents

- Get the children to make a list of the names of all the cats and dogs belonging to people in their class. How many are names that can be used for people, too?

- Ask the children to make up six dog names and six cat names. Which are the favourites?

- With the children, make a pile of pretend yummy scrummy crunchies from rolled-up scraps of paper. Make a pile of pretend fishy nibbles from cardboard cut into the shape of fish. Then get two bowls. In pairs, the children role play being either Albert or Sarah Jane and take it in turns to throw their food into the bowls. The child who gets the most food in the bowls is the winner.

- Discuss the following questions with the children: Why did Albert want to eat Sarah Jane's food? How would they describe him and his behaviour?

- Do the children think that Albert was really asleep when Sarah Jane came in to tell him off? Have they ever pretended they're asleep when they weren't? Why?

- Ask the children if they think Sarah Jane was right to go and live next door?

- In pairs, ask the children to act the story out as a play. One child takes the role of Sarah Jane, and the other, Albert. Encourage the children to sound as much like a dog or cat as they can, and to move like the animals. Afterwards, discuss how it felt to be the characters. Then reverse the roles.

- Tell the story from Albert's point of view. For example, you could start, "Hello. My name's Albert and I'm a dog…" The children can join in and contribute to the story as it progresses.

- Then tell the story from Sarah Jane's point of view.

- Do the children think Albert had changed by the end of the story? If so, why did he change?

- Have the children ever taken something that belonged to someone else? Why? What happened?

- Has anyone ever taken something that belonged to any of the children, without asking? What happened? How did the children feel?

- Have the children ever fallen out with a friend, for some other reason? What happened? How did they feel? Did they go back to being friends again? Did somebody say sorry? Do they find it hard to say sorry?

- Make a set of letter cards using the letters from the names 'Albert' and 'Sarah Jane'. Muddle up the letters from 'Albert', and see how many different words the children can make, e.g. at, art, beat, late. Do the same with the name 'Sarah Jane', and see if the children can make more words. Then put all the letters from both names together and see how many words the children can make. Can they get twenty words?